THE DOG

Text copyright © 2017 by Helen Mixter
Illustrations copyright © 2017 by Margarita Sada

17 18 19 20 21 5 4 3 2 1

Greystone Books Ltd.
greystonebooks.com

Cataloguing data available from Library and
Archives Canada
ISBN 978-1-77164-271-2 (cloth)
ISBN 978-1-77164-272-9 (epub)

Jacket and interior design by Tania Craan
Jacket illustration by Margarita Sada
Printed and bound in China on ancient-forest-friendly
paper by 1010 Printing International Ltd.

We gratefully acknowledge the support of the Canada
Council for the Arts, the British Columbia Arts Council,
the Province of British Columbia through the Book
Publishing Tax Credit, and the Government of Canada
for our publishing activities.

Canada

THE DOG

words by **Helen Mixter**

pictures by **Margarita Sada**

GREYSTONE BOOKS

Vancouver/Berkeley

When she saw me
for the first time,
she wagged her tail.

When I felt shy she sat
right next to me.

When I couldn't sleep
I could hear her breathing.

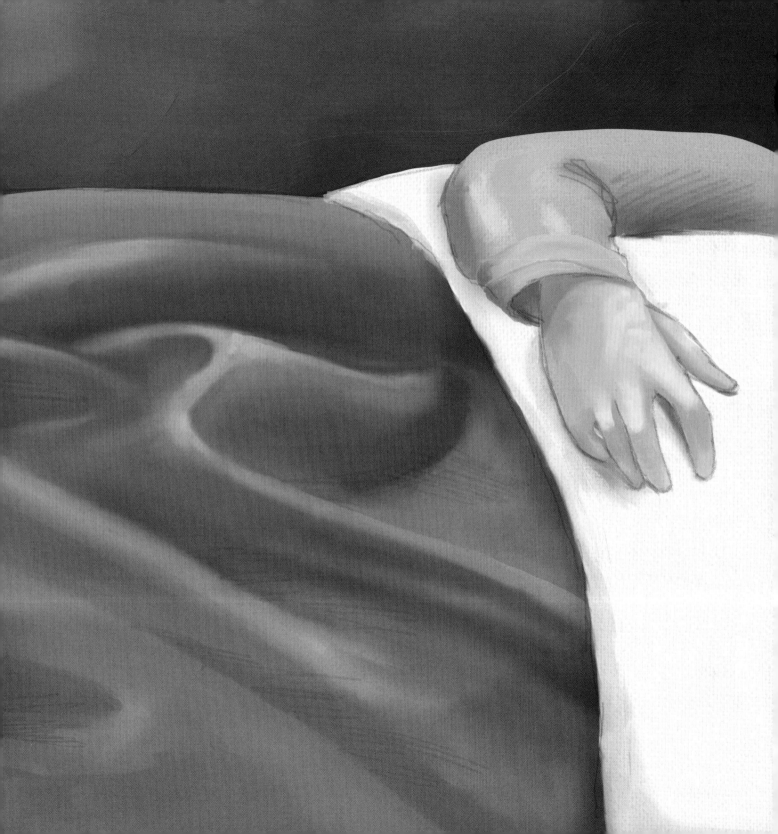

When I felt sad
I patted her and
she liked it.

When I cried
she licked
my face.

When I wanted to play in the garden
she ran and picked up the ball I threw.

When I laughed she rolled over
and waved her feet in the air.

When we went for a walk
she came with us.

When my mom read
to me and my sister
she listened to the story.

When I felt bad she knew.

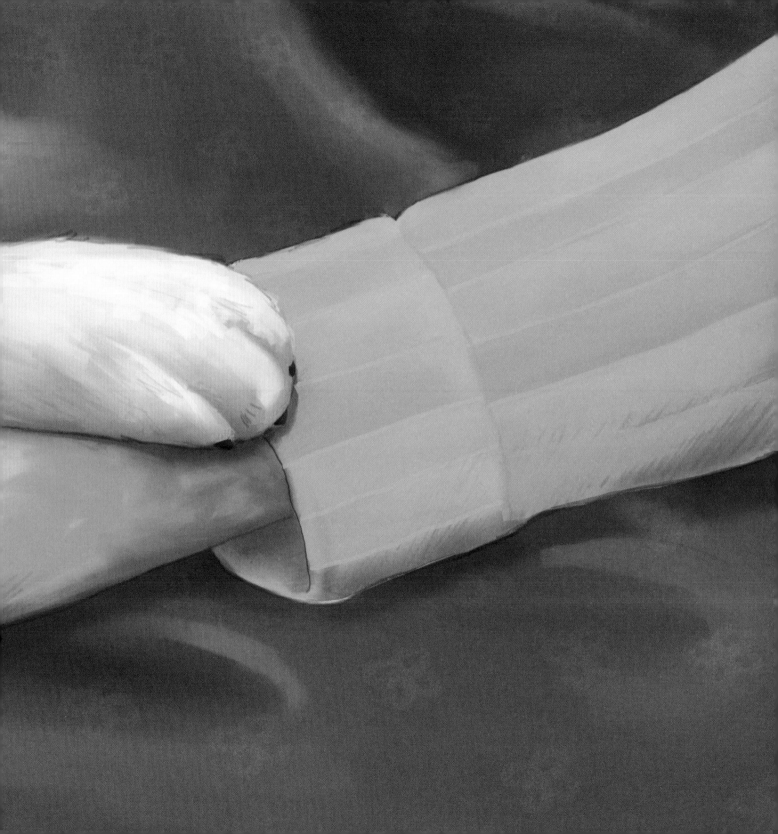

When I was tired she looked
at me with her loving eyes.

When I went to sleep
she was beside me.

PUBLISHER'S NOTE
This book was inspired by a visit to Canuck Place Children's
Hospice in Vancouver, Canada, where Poppy the therapy dog
is a companion to children with life-threatening illnesses,
their families, and the hospice's clinical care team.

Partial proceeds from sales of this book will benefit
Canuck Place Children's Hospice.
canuckplace.org